90- 325

W9-CNB-503

For Tom and Moppet   J.T.

For Emily Marshall and Trixie   R.C.

Macmillan Publishing Company
866 Third Avenue, New York, NY 10022
First published 1987 in Great Britain by Walker Books Ltd, London
First American Edition 1988
Printed and bound by L.E.G.O., Vicenza, Italy

10 9 8 7 6 5 4 3 2 1

Library of Congress Cataloging-in-Publication Data
Taylor, Judy, date.
My cat.
Summary: A little boy describes the activities of his cat
from the time she is a kitten until she has kittens of her own.
[1. Cats—Fiction] I. Cartwright, Reg, ill. II. Title.
PZ7.T21476My 1988   [E]   87-15267
ISBN 0-02-782473-X

My Cat

Written by
Judy Taylor

Illustrated by
Reg Cartwright

MACMILLAN PUBLISHING COMPANY
New York

My cat came as a kitten...

and she was beautiful.

My cat soon got to know me. .

and I played with her.

My cat lapped up her milk...

and grew stronger.

My cat was chased
up a tree...

and got stuck there.

My cat scratched our best chair…

and was scolded.

My cat caught a mouse...

and then lost it.

My cat slept all day...

and then went prowling.

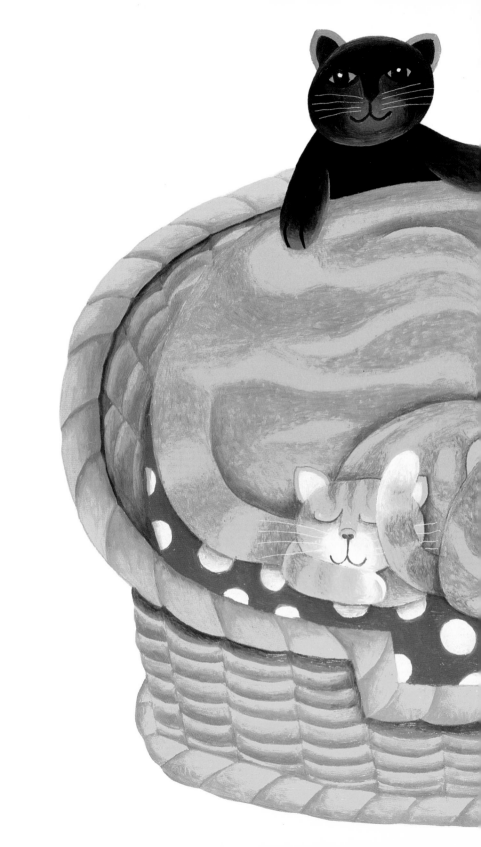

My cat had four tiny kittens...
and she loved them.